Louie loves his little sister

Yves Got

Louie's little sister
is really sweet.

She dresses up as a princess in a green and yellow dress.

First published in Great Britain in 2002
by Zero To Ten Limited
327 High Street, Slough,
Berkshire, SL1 1TX

Copyright © Yves Got 2000
English text by Simona Sideri
copyright © 2002 Zero to Ten Limited
Originally published under the title of
La petite sœur de DIDOU
by Albin Michel Inc., France, in 2000
All rights reserved.

A CIP catalogue record for this book is available from the British Library.

ISBN 1-84089-248-X

Printed and bound in Asia

She sings beautifully.
"Tra... la la... la laaaa!"

She likes to watch
Louie's puppet shows.

She's good at playing hide and seek.

She loves mashed carrots.

Sometimes she's really silly...

And sometimes she's really mean.

But even when she's naughty,
Louie still loves her.